A Dog Called Dirt

First Edition

Written and Illustrated by:

Patricia Moser Hogg

Published by Foxsong Publishing

A Dog Called Dirt

Published by Foxsong Publishing

Copyright © 2001 Patricia Moser Hogg

Cover Design by Gary Bowden of Silk Design Company
Editing: Janeile Cannon
Page Layout and Editing: Susan Luzenski
Illustrations: Patricia Moser Hogg

Foxsong Publishing
1769 Pine Creek Circle
Haslett, MI 48840
877-339-6918

ISBN 0-9677000-4-3

Library of Congress Catalog Card Number: 2001094031

Printed in the United States of America

To Dr. Edmund Visger, D.V.M.

and

Dr. Mary Sist, D.V.M.

Who took such loving care of the pets of Hoggwilde

Table of Contents

Prologue

Sometimes, even years after he disappeared, we would come into the driveway late at night, and a trick of the corner streetlight would make a large dark irregular patch by the porch pillar, just where he always used to wait for us. And for a moment, until we realized that it was just a shadow, our hearts would plummet as we whispered, "Oh, my God! He's come back!"

The Prettiest Puppy In The World
or
Looks Can Be Deceiving

Chapter One

His mother had been purportedly, a fancy show dog, "a six-hundred-dollar poodle." Our daughter, Franny, told us that the chum whose mother owned this fabulous animal was willing to give us one of her new pups. On his arrival, it was immediately obvious that the pup's father hadn't been a six-hundred-dollar show poodle. It was never determined exactly what his father was. However, he was the prettiest little puppy we had ever seen. He had a coat of silky soft black waves, a natty white mustache and goatee, and white tips on his cute little toes. Our four children promptly named him "Dirk" after their father's best friend, a dapper artist who sported a white goatee and mustache in the early sixties before facial hair had become fashionable.

I had always been dubious about naming pets after living human friends, and tried to discourage the practice. A pet's early demise, or even worse, the possibility of the friend dying before the pet did, could lead to disconcerting remarks. Also, the pet's developing personality might later embarrass the namesake. I was voted down, and the pup was christened "Dirk." The events of later years proved that the family should have respected my misgivings.

By the time our dog had reached his first birthday, most of the people in town thought his name was "Dirt." He earned that name fairly and all by himself. But whatever names the neighbors on High Street and the other citizens of Williamston adopted for him, our family always carefully referred to him as "Dirk." We did not like to admit how far off our name-bestowing instincts were.

He did not become a very large dog, and he did look like an almost-poodle. The long fringe of hair hanging over his face nearly concealed the fact that his eyes were very close together, and that his nose was much too long. His tail had not been docked. He walked with a high prancing gait, head and tail in the air, and often took a show-dog stance, which looked mighty ridiculous combined with his scruffy exterior.

It soon became evident that he was very intelligent. The children taught him a number of tricks. For a little piece of process cheese, which he would have scorned if it had been put in his food dish, he would, on the proper command, hop around on his hind legs, "sit", "roll-over", "speak" in a strained squeak, or perform his silliest stunt: ordered to "get it," he would chase his tail until he caught it, and then, while holding it in a death grip, roll his eyes in our direction.

He thought doing tricks was fun for a few months, but then it became tiresome. He developed abbreviated versions, especially when asked to "roll over." He would move close to a wall, lie down, and *try* to roll over, only to be stopped in mid-roll by that inconvenient wall. Then he would stick out his tongue and roll his eyes, "Look folks, I want to roll over, but I can't, see?" Eventually, all one had to say was, "Tricks, Dirk!" and he would go through his whole routine in five seconds – providing you had that bit of cheese in your hand, of course.

There was only one time in his life when he showed any enthusiasm for the "roll over" trick. When he was about two years old, we kept another dog, "Snoopy," for a month in the winter, while Snoopy's family vacationed in Florida. We were afraid the two little male dogs would fight at first, and kept Dirk shut in a separate room for three days. He knew, of course, another dog was in the house, and steadily yelped his anxiety. Then our eldest son, Andy, and his friend Mark staged a confrontation. Mark held Snoopy's collar and Andy held Dirk's, and the two dogs were allowed to sniff and nudge and mutter at each other for a few minutes. Their investigations apparently revealed possibilities for play and friendship, and soon they were romping all over the house together.

A day or so later, Andy took them both outdoors and hooked Dirk's leash to a porch pillar. Snoopy was so well-trained, or so lacking in curiosity, that he never left his own yard, and was never tied up. Finding himself in new surroundings and untethered, Snoopy trotted down the porch steps to investigate the adjoining yard area. In the ages-old dog tradition, he began to autograph everything that protruded from the snow, tree trunks, bushes, rocks, and the tires on our cars. Poor Dirk was beside himself, yanking on his chain, howling, and racing to every anointed object within his chain's radius, to re-mark and reclaim his property. In spite of this episode, the little dogs became good friends, and provided a lot of sociable entertainment for each other in the dull winter days until Snoopy's family came back to Michigan.

Snoopy could perform many doggy stunts, including Dirk's entire repertoire. Like Dirk, he hated to roll over. One afternoon, both dogs were in our twenty-three-foot long dining room, when son Chris came in with a little piece of cheese and ordered them both to roll over. He expected the usual hangdog looks and sham tricks, but both dogs immediately flopped down and began rolling. Over and over they rolled down the length of the room and then they rolled back. And they kept rolling until Chris took pity on them and signaled that they could quit. Poor little pooches! Snoopy was so anxious to please the humans in what, for all he knew, was now to be his permanent home, and Dirk wasn't at all sure that we weren't going to trade him in for this new dog!

pmh

Dog Houdini
or
Give Me Liberty or Give Me Death

Chapter Two

As he grew older, it became apparent to us that Dirk was somewhat lacking in the quality that has endeared and ennobled the canine race in the eyes of humankind since the dawn of civilization. Simply put, he liked all of us, but he saw no reason to let our wishes and convenience supercede his own ideas of a dog's proper business. He never menaced any persons that came on our property, or showed anything but an offhandedly-friendly interest in them. It is possible that he would have tried to defend us if one of us had been attacked, but thank heaven for our sakes, he was never put to the test. However, if a *dog* stepped one foot over our property line, he was in trouble, or at least in for a lot of haranguing and name-calling if Dirk happened to be tied up.

We certainly tried to keep him tied up, but this was one of the major points where Dirk's philosophies and ours did not coincide. He found it difficult if not impossible to pursue his interests and duties while tethered. The head of our family, Vick, was for nearly all of Dirk's life, a member of the City Council and Mayor of our small town, and there was a strict leash law on the books. Vick found it very embarrassing to have his personal dog running loose and getting into more kinds of trouble than all the rest of the pooches in town put together. He heard about Dirk's indiscretions from citizens and from the police. The cops would beseech him, "Now you know, Vick, it doesn't look very good to have the Mayor's dog running around. Surely if other people in town can keep their dogs tied up, you can!"

No, we couldn't keep him tied up. We tried collars. He discovered how to swell up his neck muscles while a collar was being fastened on him. He would seem to be strangling, his breath coming in hoarse gasps as the collar was buckled snugly. Checking on him an hour or so later, a family member would find that he had got his lower jaw under the collar and had it chewed half through. Or, if he wasn't interrupted at that point, he would be off about his business leaving the chewed-through collar still hanging on the chain as mute witness to how he escaped. Sometimes he managed to get a front or hind foot through the collar alongside his neck, and then the strangling noises he made weren't all theatrics.

Several collars and a cute little studded harness later, he was outfitted with a choke chain collar. Now we had him! For a few weeks, he alternately yanked on his chain until he choked, or lay in his doghouse sighing and rolling his eyes at us. Then he started escaping again, and we were again the targets of mad phone calls. We couldn't imagine how he was getting loose, until one day I happened to glance at him out of the side window. The poor pooch was obviously deathly ill. His head was hanging down, and he was shaking violently in the throes of a terrible chill. I had picked up the phone to call the vet for an emergency appointment when I noticed that his chain collar was inching downward along his neck with every shudder. I ran to the door – too late! Over the ears and down the nose, and he was free!

Sometimes to curtail his laments, we confined him in the house. Our house had five outside doors, and he found many opportunities to slip by or barrel his way through the legs of a family member who was attempting to enter or leave the house, or was answering the doorbell. There were times when one of us, wedged in a slightly opened door, would be chatting with someone standing on the porch, and he would clamber up and over our shoulders to squirm through the crack. And then, if the startled visitor didn't get out of the way fast enough, up and over *his* shoulders to get to the wide-open spaces.

So highly did Dirk prize freedom that he was willing to risk death for it. One summer morning, as I stood with son Tim gazing out a kitchen window toward the front of the house, we became aware of our dog's scruffy face peering at us around the corner of the house – from fifteen feet in the air! The answer to this startling apparition came to both of us simultaneously. I bounded through the door and off the porch to the front yard. Tim raced to the front hall and up the stairs. Someone had opened the upstairs hall window over the front porch roof, and it was short work for Dirk to go through the rusty window screen. There the fool stood on the tiny narrow sloping porch roof, judging the distance to the ground far below, and trying to make up his mind if jumping to freedom would be worth the chance of breaking a leg. While I was standing below waving my arms and yelling threats, Tim was unhooking the screen so he could grab Dirk's collar – or tail, or a leg, or whatever part of him was nearest the window. Dragged back inside, his leap from freedom foiled, possibly to his relief, he consented to relax on one of the kid's beds for the rest of the day, and hatch new plans in peace.

When he did attain freedom, we had to enlist outside help to catch him. He wouldn't let anyone in our family come within ten yards of him. He was, however, always happy to have the neighbor kids pet and play with him. And we outwitted him! We would call a non-family kid with the dog's last reported whereabouts, and offer a half-dollar for his capture and delivery. This was a large bit of cash for children in the early 1960's. While the first fifty cents always came easy, it was also the last fifty cents that particular child ever earned that way, as Dirk never trusted him again. We had to go further and further afield to find our "Judases" and finally ran out of them.

Then there were the few, the long-legged and long-winded, who tried to run him down. Only three people, Eric, Julie, and Bob, ever caught him in a foot race. They were all in top condition and prided themselves as runners. In their determination not to give in, they nearly had heart attacks as they chased him through downtown alleys and across back yards and softball fields before they were able to tackle him, truss him up, and drag him home.

On one memorable occasion, he had been dancing around our one-and-a-half acre yard for hours, with side forays to taunt the neighbors' dogs – and us. "Us" was a group of perhaps ten youths of varying ages and one mother – me. A few half-hearted dashes had been made at him when he got especially close to us, but he knew we couldn't catch him that way. We tried a new plan, using nods and hand signals because he understood

English too well for us to verbalize our planned maneuvers. Nonchalantly, we all walked away from him in different directions. He cavorted in the middle of our widening circle, yapping his defiance at our backs.

Then we all turned around and holding our arms wide, began walking slowly inward. Too late the scheme dawned on him, and he rushed to the perimeter to dart between two kids. They lunged together to cut him off. He backed off and tried dashes in several other directions, to no avail. Meanwhile the circle was getting tighter and tighter. Finally we were close enough to link hands. He knew when he was licked. With a tremendous dog sigh, he flopped to the ground and with his chin flat on the earth, waited to be collared. But we were never able to bring that one off again.

The key, of course, was to prevent him getting loose in the first place. We could not afford an eight-foot high chain link fenced pen with barbed wire strands curling along the top and a cement floor, and he made short work of lesser dog pens. He was willing and able to excavate to a depth of several feet to get under calf fence buried in the ground. He could scramble up any surface with a toehold, and one time he climbed a sheer wall.

On that occasion, the whole family was gone overnight to attend the wedding of a niece in northern Michigan. As it was quite cold, we decided to leave him in the basement. He couldn't get into much mischief down there, or get out – we thought. The part he was in had a tiny ground level window six feet from the floor, and there was nothing near it that could help him climb up to it.

When we got home late the next night, we opened the basement door and called him. Nothing came up the stairs but a blast of super-frigid air, which was pouring in the basement window, or rather, through the hole where the window had been. He had somehow managed to clamber up the wall, claw out the wood-framed window, and was somewhere racing with the moon across the frozen Michigan landscape.

We not only had no dog, we had no water, either. The temperature had gone down to twenty below zero, and all the water pipes were frozen. It was after midnight and we decided we could get along without water for the rest of the night. Vick boarded up the window hole, and we went to bed.

By the next morning, the house was warm, the pipes had thawed, and we had plenty of water. All the pipes had split, and water was rapidly filling the basement. It was Sunday, but our friendly plumbers answered the emergency call. It was a costly job, replacing all the water pipes and the city's water meter, which certainly wasn't free.

I don't remember when Dirk came home. I don't think we looked for him. I think maybe we half hoped he was frozen solid somewhere, but he wasn't

The solution to living with our dog Houdini had to be bigger and better shackles. At this point, he was squirming out of, or chewing through, only three to four collars a year. These were collars that would hold a mastiff. They were made of inch-and-a-half wide cowhide, fastened with heavy-duty steel buckles, and studded with brass. (Those brass studs saved his life once.) But even when he couldn't get out of his collar, he got loose. Sometimes our twenty-five pound dog broke his chain. We bought heavier chains. He figured out how to wind the chain around his tie-out stake and lunge and jerk until he had loosened the stake and could pull it out. If that didn't work, he simply dug the stake out of the ground. Then he would be on his way with fifteen feet of chain and the stake, too, jingling along merrily behind him.

Finally, I went to the local hardware store, and looked for the heaviest tie-out chain and stake they had — not the ones in the pet supplies department. We had gone through all they had to offer there. I found a stake that had a ground-level ring mounted on a swivel. The part that was underground was a giant corkscrew that went a foot or more deep into the earth. He couldn't dig that up, or get his chain under the swivel plate, either. Then I chose the heaviest tie-out chain they had. When I took my choices to the cash register, the puzzled proprietor asked what I intended to tie up. He said, "That's the outfit we sell to the 4-H kids to tether their horses. You folks don't have a pony, do you?"

This particular rig lasted the rest of Dirk's life. However, that does not mean that his days of freedom were over. After all, we were all busy with many projects, and he had nothing to do all day long but dream up ways to outwit us. I am embarrassed to admit it, but he often did.

pmh

Puppy Love
or
A Dog's Gotta Do What a Dog's Gotta Do

Chapter Three

How did Dirk develop his philosophy, so foreign to the ages-old call of duty toward humans that thousands of generations of brainwashed canines have unquestioningly accepted? Undoubtedly, his Romeo daddy bequeathed him a few wild genes, but one of his early experiences may also provide a clue.

As previously stated, he was, in his young days, a beautiful, silky-coated, well-built little dog. He was *cute!*

One of our friends had a female "cockerpoo." This was the breed, which, for lack of any better information, was usually assigned to Dirk. The friend wanted to breed her cockerpoo with ours. We took Dirk to their country home at the appropriate time and he was shut up for a whole week in a garage with their seductive and experienced little lady dog. He was really too young for what was required of him, but with her help he figured it out. He was a very happy and enlightened dog when we brought him home.

Although we didn't realize it at the time, he had found his purpose in life – and in the fourteen years he spent on this earth, he never lost sight of the quest. We have no idea how many of his progeny prance about the countryside to this day. To our certain knowledge, he actually consummated only two other relationships. We only found out about them from the big fuss people made. We are sure, though, that never again was he put up for a week in a luxury hotel, so to speak, with a lady. He must have been puzzled later that the activity which was encouraged that week by all the humans around him was later rewarded with tongue-lashings and thrown bricks. No matter, he kept chasing his dream. Indeed, we suspected that calls to romance wafting to him on the breeze from the far side of town may have instigated his most determined and crafty escapes.

Sometimes he didn't have to go very far. Next door lived the hardworking, hard-nosed, and hard-talking landlady of a big old house that had been converted to apartments. In anticipation of her teenaged son's upcoming college expenses, she had purchased a purebred cocker spaniel, which she intended to breed periodically with another blue-blooded spaniel. She calculated that the sale of the pups would pay her son's college fees each year.

Neither she nor her son was handy with tools, and she habitually cut corners on materials. They built a flimsy orange-crate doghouse, and put a pen around it which had 1" x 2"s for the corner posts and gateposts. Then they tacked chicken wire around the posts. The "gate" was an ancient rusted screen door. The pen did keep the spaniel in – she was a dumb and spiritless pooch – but when love beckoned, it didn't keep our dog out for more than twenty seconds. I hadn't realized that the neighbor's cocker spaniel was a girl, much less that Dirk had discovered that fact, made his escape, and was over there, when a tremendous pounding on our back door and bellows of rage alerted me to the possibility that somebody in our household must have done *something*.

Our neighbor was the door-pounder and she was nearly speechless. "Your - your - your - god - *god* -

goddam - DOG!!!" she gargled. I ran out the door and across the back yard. It didn't take long for me to figure out what had happened, given the tangled wreckage of the pen in the yard next door. She gave all the credit for the mess to Dirk, but at this point, he and the cocker spaniel were in the center of a joyous melee of half a dozen male mutts. I refused to take responsibility for the consequences, and as she was too thrifty to take her spaniel to the vet for a morning-after shot, eventually there was a litter of funny-looking pups. None of them bore any resemblance to Dirk, thank goodness.

A later adventure was more serious. Our dog was the sole perpetrator. One summer day when Dirk was properly tied up and resting by his doghouse, I was standing on the front sidewalk gazing idly up the street when I noticed a car cruising slowly along the curb. The driver, a very determined-looking man, was minutely scanning the lawns on both sides of the street. I had a premonition even before he suddenly stopped the car at our curb, jerked the door open, and leaped out. He was as mad as our neighbor had been but quite a bit more articulate.

Striding toward me, shaking his fists in Dirk's direction, he barked, "If I *ever* see that damn dog loose *anywhere, I'm gonna SHOOT HIM!"*

He didn't wait for me to ask what our dog had done, he *told* me. "That-cur-came-in-my-house-right-through-the-screen-door-and-and-raped-my-purebred-bassett-hound-in-the-middle-of-my-living-room-floor-and-my-kids-had-hysterics-they-thought-he-was-killing-her-and - - -!!!" Well, we don't need to describe any more of that harrowing episode.

Sometimes when Dirk had extricated himself from his shackles, he wouldn't show up for a couple of days. Then Andy would cruise the streets looking for him. Many times he found him, filthy and hungry, lying patiently in a gutter in front of the beloved's home. Being preoccupied with his impossible dream, he was usually pretty easy to collar and be chauffeured home, frustrated, tired and morose. In the years since, we have often wondered why no vet suggested neutering him, but apparently it was not a common practice at the time. That wouldn't have put a crimp in all of his activities, but at least it would have kept him out of one kind of trouble.

The last time he was definitely identified as a wooer was near the end of his long and busy life. He hadn't shown many signs of slowing down, but he had begun to seem more resigned to spending long periods basking in the sun by his doghouse.

Then one day, the siren call came and he contrived to free himself for what may have been his last romantic fling. He was absent for three or four days. I found him one morning on the dining room porch, completely exhausted. As I wished to enter the house and he was blocking the doorway, I started to boost him aside. When my foot touched him, he let out a shriek. Any attempt to move him caused him great pain, and an hour later, he seemed to be nearly paralyzed.

Time for an emergency trip to the vet with Dirk in a blanket sling. His doctor couldn't diagnose the problem, and sent us to the Michigan State University vet school clinic where they had better X-ray machines and many sophisticated testing methods. I asked that they make a thorough evaluation of his health.

After two young vets took him away, I waited tensely in the lobby for over an hour before they reappeared for a conference. They began by expressing disbelief that he was fourteen years old, as his records stated; they would have thought him, at most, only half that age. I assured them that we had owned him since he was a tiny pup.

Then they asked me what in the world we fed him to keep him in such good shape. I said he had grown up with cats and had eaten cat food all his life; he refused to eat dog food. They pondered this for a few moments. Then they asked me when had he been shot.

"SHOT!!?"

"Yes, Ma'am, he has been shot several times. The x-rays show three different sizes of shot in him."

I pondered that for a few moments. Finally, I asked them if they had determined what was ailing him this time. They said he had a *severely sprained back*. They had given him painkillers and a muscle relaxant, and provided more medicine for us to give him later. Soon we were on our way home again, and after a few days of rest and medication, he was only slightly creaky.

Not long after, I was visiting a neighbor up the street, and audibly wondered how a dog could sprain his back that bad. She said it didn't surprise her. She told me that her neighbor in the next house had acquired a female St. Bernard, and Dirk had spent most of a week trying to consummate a relationship with that dog.

I said, "Why in heck didn't you call and tell us to come and get him?" She blushed and said that the spectacle had been quite interesting for the folks on that end of the street. In fact, I gathered they were *betting* on whether he was going to be able to do it or not. I asked the St. Bernard's owner if she wasn't worried that her dog might be preggers, and she answered, "Que será será!"

But apparently he didn't connect, as no little "Bernapoos" ever put in an appearance.

Adventures in Grooming

or

A Dog By Any Other Name Would Smell As Bad

Chapter Four

By the time Dirk was two years old, he had settled into a comfortable lifestyle that expressed his personality. His doghouse suited him perfectly. It was an old wooden herring barrel stuffed with straw, lying on its side. Dirk liked to burrow into the straw, and inhale the lingering fishy ambience of his little home. By this time, we were putting up a losing battle in regard to grooming him. He was a dog of his day — the hippie/love child/free spirit era. We tried to bathe and brush him on a regular basis and clip out the mats which formed in his fine soft poodle fur, but he didn't like any of it and his protests grew progressively more forceful.

In the bathroom his yells were deafening as he struggled and floundered in the tub. The bathroom would be drenched by his thrashings; even the ceiling would be splattered. When the designated bathers had finally had all they could stand, they would attempt to blot the dog if there were any towels left in the bathroom that were not soaking wet. Then Dirk would be released to race into the living room and leap into a low wicker chair, where he could roll and rub himself damp-dry on the cushions. At this point, he would be removed from the house and tied up near his doghouse. His chain was long enough that he could usually find several substances in its radius that would help him smell right again. Included, of course, would be his own excrement, any bits of decayed vegetable matter and animal flesh near his food bowl, and if the boys had been working on their cars, he was close enough to that area to wallow in the nice greasy dirt and add a little "Eau de Mechanics Shoppe" to his bouquet. We persisted in these unwelcome periodic cleanups, although half an hour later, nobody but his shampoo team could tell the difference in his before-and-after-bath appearance and aroma.

However, a smell he contracted on one occasion was definitely not his fault, and he didn't like it any better than we did. We had many non-human residents in our large yard, which included orchard trees, a big vegetable garden, wild woodsy and brush-covered areas, boulders and piles of smaller rocks, and a marshy riverbank. There were many confrontations between our pets and our yard's other residents which included 'possums, raccoons, woodchucks, squirrels, and a tribe of rabbits that appeared, by their very large size and odd white spots, to have interbred with tame white bunnies that had escaped.

There was also a pair of skunks that lived under daughter Franny's old playhouse. Every summer evening around eleven o'clock, they took a constitutional around the house, announcing their stately progress by a slight but not offensive odor that floated into one open window after another as they passed. Occasionally, late at night, a family member might walk past the seldom-used front porch and notice the two of them enjoying the view of the street light from the top step. They bothered nobody and we certainly took great care not to bother them.

However, one night about midnight when the household was fast asleep, it became evident that they *had* been bothered. The house quickly filled with a gas so thick and powerful, it caused throats to constrict and eyes to water. This is not a pleasant way to be awakened. In a few minutes we had identified Dirk as the skunk's target. He acted guilty, embarrassed, confused, and overwhelmed. As he was tied up that night, it couldn't have been his fault – or not much, anyway. We deduced that the skunks had been attracted to his food dish, which contained remnants of his evening meal: nice, smelly, fishy cat food. We thought the skunks must have attempted to raid his food dish, and that he objected and the skunks won the argument.

Given the certainty of no sleep or being gassed in our beds, there was no question of waiting till the next day to de-skunk the dog. Dirk had to submit to every skunk-odor remedy we had ever heard of that night. By morning, the house was aired out pretty well, and the dog wasn't unduly repellent. As he was by that time too unmanageable to clip without being tranquilized, and old enough to make using tranquilizers life-threatening, he had to continue to wear his anointed coat. For over a year, whenever the weather was damp, traces of a faint mephitic fragrance wafted about him.

For several years, he had an annual late spring haircut to get rid of the three-inch-thick mats of winter wool that covered him like slabs of mattress. I don't recall that he ever had any fleas. Either the mats of hair were too dense for fleas to penetrate or his axle-grease and doggie poop smell convinced them that his blood would be inedible. Shearing him was quite an undertaking. The unpopular chore took two people half a day to complete. One Hogg child would wrestle the portion of Dirk's body that was being worked on into position, while the other one carefully snipped off his felted coat and tried not to nick his skin. Eventually, Dirk objected so violently to getting a haircut that we had to resort to getting a tranquilizer from the vet to give him on clipping day. The tranquilizer made things a lot easier for everyone, including Dirk. The process could be confined to one spot out by the garden, which, though it looked afterward as though a scene of bloodless dismemberment had taken place there, was a better outcome than having hair tufts decorating the entire yard where his lunges had taken him and his barbers.

Strange things were sometimes found in the pile of poodle clippings. Once, Franny found a little frog skeleton. We assumed that Dirk had rolled in a ripe frog in the spring – although it *could* have been alive at the time – and it had somehow adhered to his fuzz. Efficient little scavenger beetles had consumed the carcass, and nothing was left but the delicate bones.

After Dirk's vet had said that he was so old another tranquilizer dose might kill him, the spring haircutting ritual ceased and he went natural, as God had no doubt intended. But we never stopped looking for solutions to the grooming problem. One day, in the current issue of our science magazine, we read about a new drug that was being tested by our own Michigan State University's Agriculture Department. Experiments were being made with a newly developed chemical, which could revolutionize sheep shearing. The day the drug was administered to a sheep, each hair cell born that day in its individual follicle would be very weak.

When several months had passed and the sheep's wool had reached the desired depth, the shepherd could grasp the animal's coat and neatly peel the fleece off like an orange rind. The chemical had so far produced no adverse reactions in sheep.

Over the dinner table, our family discussed the process and what a boon it could be to people who owned woolly longhaired dogs. Franny had her driver's license by then, and the next afternoon, without notifying any family members of their intentions, she and Tim drove to MSU. They sought out the right department of the Ag School and were allowed to see and talk to the people who were conducting the experiments. They wanted to know if it would be possible to obtain some of the drug to try on their dog. The startled scientists said that nobody had tested it on dogs, and they had never thought of such an application. It seemed to be safe for sheep, but who knew how it might affect dogs? Franny and Tim persisted. They were offering their dog as a test case. The scientists' refusal was flat and firm. They seemed, indeed, to be actually repelled by the unnatural children who had no thought for their beloved pet's welfare. Actually, perhaps it didn't work too well on sheep, either, in the long run, as we never read any subsequent articles about the process.

Before baths had been abandoned as useless, one hot summer day Franny and Tim, attempting to bypass the extensive bathroom cleanup that was necessary after Dirk's indoor baths, were giving him a scrub down in an old washtub outdoors. During the wild and noisy ablutions, they discussed a plan to change his appearance by bleaching some white spots with peroxide in his charcoal-colored fur. Dirk had been having some run-ins with the town cops lately, and Franny and Tim thought the white spots might make him less identifiable.

They were too busy to notice an Arm of the Law walking up behind them to the porch, bringing Vick's City Council meeting agenda papers, until he said, "Forget it, kids, there's *nothing* you could do to that dog so we wouldn't recognize him!"

However, once in his life he was not only rendered unrecognizable to his buddies, the family cats, he couldn't even recognize himself. One summer Franny saved up enough from her first job to get him a professional "do." One look at him and the salon owner doubled her price. No matter, it was worth it; the shop really did a magnificent job on him. When Franny brought him home, he had been neatly shaved, had had a flea bath, and been sprayed with a powerfully perfumed deodorant. He had always appeared to be a stocky little dog with big feet, but the pooch that descended hesitantly from the car was quite small and had narrow neat little feet. Every hair between his toes, hanging over his beady little eyes, and covering his longish ears had been clipped. The only hairs left on his body that were longer than a quarter of an inch were a few silly fronds at the end of his tail, the salon owner's half-hearted attempt at a sort of poodle style. He walked uncertainly to the house, and was coaxed up the porch steps and into the dining room – where he was immediately set upon and walloped all over the floor by three cats who had no intention of allowing an intruder into Dirk's territory.

At this point, he was obviously suffering from a severe identity crisis. If he looked, felt, and smelled so different that even the cats didn't know him, who was he? When we reached down to pat and reassure him, the touch of our hands literally sent him straight up. He shuddered wildly and his skin twitched. We began to realize that the insulation he had carried on his body all his life had prevented him from feeling many of our caresses.

Soon the embarrassed kitties recognized him again, and came up to salute him in their fashion, winding around his legs and trailing their tails across his face. A few days later, the last of the doggie deodorant perfume had evaporated and he had replaced it with his own preferred blend. But he remained somewhat morose and depressed, as any hippie would, until his hair grew to a respectable length again. During this period he attracted a few fleas, and we could always tell when one had bitten him by his violent twitch and surprised yelp. That was his one and only experience with professional grooming.

Dirk not only despised grooming attempts on himself, on at least one occasion, he helped another dog to regain a natural odor. A nice lady in one of the apartments next door had a beautiful little Pomeranian. He was too pretty to be real; he looked like a fluffy apricot-colored toy dog. His owner liked Dirk, and occasionally invited him into her apartment where she let the two little dogs romp together and fed them cookies. It's a good thing she was so tolerant and liked dogs so much, if the story another neighbor told us later was true. The lady had bathed and groomed her pretty pooch, decked him out in his rhinestone-studded collar, and put blue bows behind his ears. Then she tied him to her porch pillar while she finished preparations for a planned visit to friends. All dressed to go, she got to her door just in time to see Dirk trotting around her little dog, smelling him all over. Then he lifted his leg and drenched the gorgeous but unnatural creature.

We are sure that Dirk felt he had provided a real service to his fluffy friend. We don't know what the other dog thought. His mistress seems to have had an incredible sense of humor. By report, she laughed till the tears came. Then she changed her clothes and re-shampooed her Pomeranian.

The Canine World is All that Counts
or
Good Old Boys

Chapter Five

Dirk seemed to be fond of all of us, but the concerns of the human race didn't figure largely in his scheme of things, except as impediments to dog society. He was a dog's dog, and his standing in the canine world was really all that mattered to him. What with his talent for freeing himself and his bent for roaming, it is safe to say that Dirk was undoubtedly acquainted with most of the dogs in town at any given time. That is not to say that he was especially friendly with them, with the exception of lady dogs at certain seasons. He enjoyed flaunting his freedom and driving tied-up dogs wild by trespassing on their property and flinging insults at them, stealing their toys, and peeing all over the trees and bushes just out of reach of their tethers.

The two dogs he most enjoyed pestering lived near the end of our street. They were big strong hunting dogs, considered very valuable by their owners, and normally kept chained to their large, luxurious kennel. One winter, we noticed that Dirk, after an hour or so on the loose, would occasionally come trotting into the yard carrying in his mouth a brightly-colored plastic bowl of the type in which oleomargarine was sold. Dirk would lie down in the snow with the bowl between his paws, and gnaw at the congealed contents. We didn't think much about it, even though on a walk up the street, I had noticed that the Ellis dogs had the same kind of bowls. But everyone had these utilitarian items, and quite often they were used as pet dishes.

It was a long snowy winter, but spring came at last with a sudden thaw, and our yard overnight was abloom with what appeared to be oversized crocuses, gold, blue, and lilac. We counted seventeen of the oleo containers. We thought they might belong to the Ellis family, but were too embarrassed to ask.

Our uneasy suspicion that the bowls belonged to the Ellis dogs, seemed to be confirmed one day when they got loose and came looking for their dinner dishes, preferably with a pound or two of dog flesh included. From the kitchen windows, I saw the two big hounds trotting with a grim purpose into our yard. Dirk was tied up, and he seemed to sense they hadn't come for fun and games. He gave one desperate yelp and after that, he was too busy to holler. The dogs got him down and rolled him over. While one was earnestly attempting to tear through Dirk's matted wool as a first step toward disemboweling him, the other one was going for his jugular, but was temporarily hampered by our dog's brass-studded cowhide collar.

I really don't remember what happened next, but it became one of the kids' favorite "Mom stories." They say I grabbed a heavy industrial broom off the porch and fearlessly kicked my way into the battle, bellowing and clubbing the interlopers with the broom. They were most impressed that I broke the thick solid oak broom handle over the back of the hound that was gnawing on Dirk's midriff. That got his attention, and he seemed to lose interest in ripping our dog's tummy open. The other one wasn't making much headway against the brass-studded collar, either. With what poise they could muster, they disengaged themselves and trotted back up the sidewalk homewards, with me screaming after them and dusting their rumps with half a broom. Dirk, the fool, leaped to his feet, shrieking swear words and taunts at their tails. Maybe he gained a little sense of caution, though, as he never brought home any more oleo bowls. Or maybe their owners got some dog food dishes they could anchor down.

Apparently all dogs, when at liberty, enjoy the illusion that they could live off the land if they had to. Even the most pampered show dog is a scavenger at heart. Dirk, who was at large rather frequently, seldom came back home without a souvenir of some sort: a dried-up carp from the riverbank; a piece of a deer foreleg with the hoof still on it; a woodchuck that we re-interred three times in as many weeks before Dirk got tired of digging it up again – or most likely, it just disintegrated. These were among his most memorable finds. Of course, there was much more of a garbage-pail variety: sandwich wrappers and bread bags containing a few slices blue with mold; paper bags stuffed with greenish eggshells, coffee grounds, rotten onions and potato peelings. In fact, anything that could once be classified as food, but had since been relegated to a garbage can, attracted him. Ingesting anything he personally dragged home was a firm tenet of his adventurous nature, and the more disgusting the substance was, the more he appeared to relish it. His favorite spot to sample new gourmet experiences was the middle of the front yard by the sidewalk; that is where he reduced the soggy brown paper bags and wax paper wrappings to confetti.

One bright fall morning, he scavenged the prize trophy of his life. Looking out the front window, I was appalled to see that he had a large bundle wrapped in freezer paper on the ground in front of him, and was working at the tape and string that bound it. I went out to investigate, but as I tried to get close enough to see what he had, he growled at me. When I reached for the package, he rolled his eyes and snarled, and it wasn't just a polite warning. He was so excited about his find that he was trembling, and he didn't intend to give up his package without a fight. As far as I know, that was the only time in his life that he ever threatened to bite anyone.

I did get close enough to read the black grease-penciled label. It gave the information that the package contained several pounds of spareribs. From the pristine condition of the paper bundle, I doubted it had ever seen the inside of a garbage can. I had a mental vision of that package of ribs being left to thaw on an insecure back porch in preparation for a barbeque party for ten people that evening. I had no idea who the meat belonged to; I just hoped to hell that if anyone saw Dirk steal it, that person didn't recognize him as the Hogg dog.

Dirk was getting nervous. With me standing there waving my arms and yelling at him, he couldn't fully savor the delightful preliminaries of shredding the wrappings to get at the first delectable taste of stolen raw meat. He got to his feet, managed to get the heavy package in his jaws, and with his head thrown back as much as possible to balance it, he walked carefully out of the yard. He had negotiated only about fifty feet of sidewalk before a husky black Lab trotting down the street veered over to investigate. Dirk tried to accelerate, but he was overloaded. His neck was beginning to tire with the weight of the meat, and as I watched, his head dropped lower and lower until the white package was scraping the ground. Frantically he tried clamping his teeth on one corner of the precious bundle and dragging it. The black Lab quickly overtook him, and the tug of war lasted but a few seconds. Then the big dog hefted the parcel in his capacious mouth and was off, presumably in the direction of his own home, followed by Dirk, who was howling with frustration.

Dirk and the black Lab were not the only dogs in town enjoying liberty that day. Before the Lab had gone half a block, as I watched, another mutt caught up with him, and the same scenario was played out. The Lab tried to put on a burst of speed, but his head was sagging noticeably. The other dog grabbed the package and ran off with Dirk and the Lab both after him.

An hour or so later, an exhausted Dirk came home to rest on the porch, so crestfallen that he put up no resistance to being tied up. Perhaps he was mulling over the possibility that if he had stayed in our yard, other dogs might have been uneasy about trying to snatch food from his jaws on his own turf, but by dog rules as soon as he crossed his home boundaries, he was fair game.

That was not the end of the story. I had several errands to do all over town, and it seemed that everywhere I went, I saw the same package of spareribs being carried by a different dog that was struggling to hold up its head and stay in front of an ever-increasing pack of canine followers. The wrappings were no longer crisp and white; they were tattered and muddy and dog-slobbered, but still more or less intact. All day long, no dog had been allowed the few minutes of peace necessary to unwrap and savor the flavor of that first lovely meaty rib-bone!

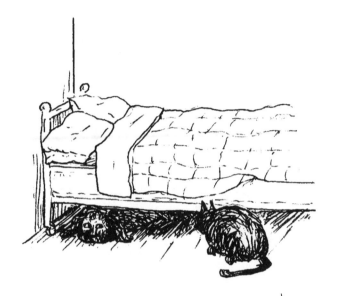

Cats Are Okay in Their Place
or
Some of My Best Friends are Felines

Chapter Six

On the whole, Dirk seemed to prefer cats to his fellow canines. He had very good relations with our cats. They amicably shared food dishes and sleeping spots. On chilly days, they all curled up together on the sunniest porch. During much of Dirk's life, the cats of the family were Little Georgie, a sweet-natured gold chrysanthemum of a Persian cat; Hodge, a nervous black Siamese with so many brains they often got in the way of his cat instincts; and Moxie.

Moxie was one of the most remarkable and interesting animals we were ever to know. By the time Dirk came into the family, Moxie was the king of all the neighborhood cats *and* dogs. He was a very large and burly black cat, although perhaps not quite as large and burly as he thought he was. His many fights and a chronic ear infection had given him an arresting physiognomy. One eye was white with a cataract. His much-chewed ears were puckered and notched. In a run-in with a raccoon or woodchuck, his chin had nearly been torn off. The vet had managed to patch him up and the flesh eventually grew back to his jawbone in a tenuous fashion. Because of the jaw injury, he couldn't quite close his mouth, and much of the time his tongue was hanging out. He was often badly injured in one of his conflicts with other cats or the wildlife in the backyard, and then the fever and stress would cause most of his hair to fall out temporarily.

Moxie had been neutered at a fairly young age to curb his fighting and wandering, but the procedure didn't curb his activities much. After the operation, he didn't go looking for trouble seasonally anymore; he fought all year round just for the fun of it. He was a mighty hunter, concentrating on full-sized rabbits and the big rats that inhabited the neighborhood woodpiles.

Much of his time was spent sitting on a porch railing where he could survey the neighborhood with his one good eye. He knew to the inch where the property line was around our L-shaped yard. When a dog that didn't belong to us stepped over the line, Moxie would descend from his perch and approach the trespasser with the deliberate rolling gait of a miniature black bear. As this Long John Silver of the cat world, white eye gleaming, snaggled fangs in view, and ears not like those of other cats, maintained his steady ponderous tread dogward, the stoutest-hearted cat-hating canine would be assailed by a strange doubt. "Does this cat know something I don't know?" would seem to be the thought behind the puckered doggy brow.

At this point, the wise dog would decide to quietly sidle out of the yard. The foolhardy one would charge. Moxie never flinched or faltered. He stood his ground and –snicker-snee! The dog had a new nasal passage! Trailing blood and screams, the intruder would high tail it for the south side of town, still not sure that was a *cat* he had tangled with.

Moxie was not a dog-hater, and he truly seemed to be fond of Dirk. Of course, he had trained Dirk from earliest puphood to be properly respectful. Only twice that we remember did Dirk step over the line, and the first time it was inadvertently. He had been freed from one of the detested baths, and as was his habit, he raced into the living room to roll himself dry in his favorite cushioned wicker chair. Out of sight, from Dirk's point of view, Moxie was curled up in the chair cushions enjoying a peaceful siesta. Too late for Dirk to check his headlong gallop, Moxie lifted his head and peered over the cushion with his awful white-eyed glare. Dirk put on the brakes; his feet and claws scrambled and skidded on the slick floor, as with a frightened yelp, he crashed into the chair. Moxie was a very intelligent cat. He realized the poor pooch hadn't purposely intended to slam into him, but for disciplinary reasons, he still felt he had to administer a couple of sharp slaps on the snout. Then he went back to sleep again, and Dirk crept upstairs to recover his nerves.

Dirk, with his rebellious spirit and dislike of submitting to anybody else's rules, couldn't help but have a teensy bit of suppressed resentment toward Moxie. One summer morning, he got his chance to retaliate. A strange dog wandered into the yard, and spying Moxie, decided a good quick cat chase would be just the thing to enliven a dull day. Moxie, on guard as usual, calmly stepped down the porch steps and stalked purposefully toward the intruder. At this point, a second mutt trotted up and decided to join the fun. A single dog of any size or breed could never faze Moxie, nor had he any intention of running from two dogs. Changing his position slightly, he was warily sizing up his opponents and planning his strategy. Suddenly, Dirk, who had been flanking Moxie and yelling threats at the marauders, saw the chance of a lifetime. He charged Moxie, too.

Moxie was brave, but not foolhardy. "He who fights and runs away will live to fight another day."

With three canines snapping at his tail, he streaked across the yard to a tall elm, and in a matter of seconds was established in a comfortable crotch forty feet above the ground. The dogs yammered and shrieked and jumped against the tree trunk until they were tired of the game. Then, well pleased with themselves, they trotted to their respective homes for lunch, and Dirk also decided to take a break in the house and cadge a few sandwich bites.

Moxie stayed in the elm tree for a couple of hours, grooming himself carefully and thinking about things. Then he rappelled himself down the tree trunk, and entered the house. Once indoors, he began his search with a grim purpose. He soon located the unsuspecting traitor, who had all but forgotten what had been just several minutes of rousing good fun for him. Moxie walked up to him and deliberately pierced his ear with a newly honed claw. Yelping, Dirk fled through the house and found refuge under an upstairs bed, where Moxie kept him prisoner for a half hour or so.

Moxie wasn't through with him yet. He stalked the poor dog remorselessly for three days. Dirk didn't feel safe anywhere. Every time he began to hope that Moxie had found something more interesting to do, the dreadful white eye would peer at him from a different doorway; from behind a wastebasket; leering from the top of the refrigerator. The infernal black beast could be blending with the shadows under the car, or even be lurking in Dirk's personal doghouse. Dirk was nearly a nervous wreck before Moxie decided he had learned his lesson, and would never attempt such a foolish stunt again. And so far as we know, he never did.

Christmas is for Everyone
or
Dogs Have Feelings, Too

Chapter Seven

Our pets reacted in different ways to the bustle of holidays. The cats were intensely interested and participated enthusiastically in all the preparations, from the initial search for seasonal items in seldom-opened drawers and remote areas of the house, through all the manifestations and stages of the Yule festivities. Every day, new and exotic-smelling items were carried into the house, all contained in lovely crackly bags for cats to play in. Then individually, family members would secrete themselves behind closed doors and do things to these mysterious items with rustly paper and shiny ribbons to further titillate feline sensibilities. The young cats would go into excitement overdrive, rampaging through the rooms wild-eyed, with tail aloft and fur akimbo. The older cats preferred to camp out in the kitchen and watch the unusually complicated culinary operations, with only an occasional discreet rub against the cook's leg and a polite chirp as a reminder that they were always ready and willing to be of service as taste-testers.

All the cats we ever had thought that having a fresh, woodsy-smelling tree brought into the house was a wonderful idea, and each one, depending on age and disposition, had a different way of expressing their feelings. One December, little black Siamese Hodge, four months old, was so affected when the big tree was hauled up the porch that he dived into the thick branches and refused to come out. The tree was too bushy and stickery for anyone to try to retrieve him, so he stayed in it for hours, all through the operations of wrestling the tree into the house and erecting it in the big bay window.

Finally he did come out and sat in the double doorway to the dining room, across the living room from the tree. He made no attempt to join the other cats that were busily smelling the ornaments and patting them tentatively, tripping people, tangling up the strings of lights, and generally being helpful. All during the decorating process, our kitten watched closely, but stayed in the doorway.

A couple of hours later, the job was done. The decorating crew sat back to admire their creation and discuss possible refinements to the color scheme and balance by moving selected ornaments from one twig to another. Suddenly a shape that appeared to be a large black bat flew by their ears, hit the newly adorned tree about four feet from the floor, and disappeared in the foliage. The tree tottered and a rain of blown glass ornaments trickled down through the branches. People leapt to the rescue, but to no avail; the tree crashed to the floor, Hodge and all. Fortunately, it fell into the room instead of through the big windows. After it was pulled free of the bay area, the broken glass swept up, and the spilled water from the tree base mopped up, the stepladder was brought back in and a large screw eye was installed in the bay window ceiling. Then the top of that tree, and the top of every subsequent Christmas tree long after Hodge was gone was firmly wired to the ceiling.

A few years later, we had another hyper young'un, named Floyd. Uncharacteristically, he seemed to be very little interested in all rituals surrounding the arrival, installation and adornment of an eight-foot tree in his home. Through most of the procedures, he was curled up in front of a hot-air register in a distant room dozing. He must have been considering some plans, but he waited until we were all abed and fast asleep before he carried them out.

When we got up the next morning, we found that the lower three feet of the tree had been denuded. As high as Floyd could reach or jump, there was not a single ornament left on any twig. Drifts of broken colored glass in the corners of the room showed what had happened to many of them. The ones that held up to being ricocheted off the walls had been batted through a small opening where a new heating run was to be installed, and they were in the crawl space directly below. We salvaged all we could find, but for many years afterwards, every once in awhile a kitty would come upstairs carrying a trophy in its mouth from that long ago Christmas. Following that experience, every year the lower branches of our trees were festooned with "cat ornaments" made of unbreakable plastic or painted tin and wood.

Our old sedate cats loved Christmas trees. They would lie underneath, or on a nearby chair or footstool, and gaze for hours into the softly lighted boughs adorned with twinkling ornaments. There they would inhale the piney aroma, smile and purr, and lose themselves in happy meditations. On Christmas morning they would join us, cheerfully expecting something special to happen. They were always rewarded with catnip mice and little balls with bells inside, which they were allowed to unwrap themselves. In fact, it wasn't safe to put any family presents under the tree until the last minute, or the cats would have had them all unwrapped. Of course, they spent the gifting aftermath rolling and hiding in the crumpled paper and ribbons, which they thought was the most fun of all.

They enjoyed everything about Christmas, including the visits of all well-wishers and dinner guests. They felt it their duty to greet people and make them feel at home. They were convinced that all visitors loved cats, or if by chance they didn't, a short course of leg rubbings and hand kissings was all it would take to re-educate a cat hater. In order to get them out of the way, at least during the dinner hour, we would often shut them up in the basement or the studio, where they put in their time vocalizing their frustration. Occasionally, deciding that their banishment was due to the other cats' misbehavior, they would get into short, noisy free-for-alls.

To keep from having to listen to their complaints when some guests who weren't particularly crazy about cats were present for one Christmas dinner, all the cats were rounded up and shooed up the attic stairway, which was the kind that pulled down out of a hatch in the upstairs hall ceiling. They didn't need to be urged to race up the ladder-like stairs, as the attic was one of the forbidden areas of hidden secrets that they were always yearning to explore. Then – the trapdoor was shut, and they realized, too late, that it was just another jail.

As we couldn't hear them expressing their opinions two stories below, the holiday dinner proceeded merrily without any little cadgers begging for bits of turkey. Presently, one of the young guests ran upstairs on some errand, and came down to announce with a worried look, "There are cats falling out of the ceiling up there!" There were, indeed. About thirty-five pounds of cats had congregated in a pile on the end of the trapdoor, and their weight had made it swing open, dumping them nine feet to the hall floor. That was the first and only time we attempted to sequester pets in the attic.

In contrast to the cats, Dirk seemed to have so little interest in holiday preparations that nobody had ever thought to even provide a gift for him. Beyond lifting a leg by the tree if he thought he was alone and could get away with it, he couldn't have cared less had a whole forest been installed indoors. His only interest in the seasonal activities appeared to be connected with the unusual number of comings and goings, which afforded him many opportunities to slip out and go adventuring.

But one Christmas when he was seven or eight years old, his attitude changed. That year, the mother of Chris' friend Clay had made very large hard gingerbread men, elaborately decorated with icing and personalized with children's names as gifts. Chris was the recipient of one. It was wrapped in cellophane, and had a hanger on it so it could be hung as an ornament. As it was quite heavy and appeared to be almost indestructible, Chris hung it on a sturdy lower branch among the cat ornaments. Alone in the living room for a while, Dirk investigated the tree to the extent of noticing this new item. He decided to pull it off and test its edibility. He had chewed off most of one arm of the rock-hard cookie man when he was found out. Chris took it away from him, but seeing that it was ruined as a decoration, he wrapped it up and stuck it in the higher branches for a dog present.

On the big day, Dirk was watching the loud and cheerful exchange of presents from the dining room, where he was lying with his nose between his paws, apparently bored silly. Then Chris, producing the little package, exclaimed, "Why, here's one for *DIRK!*" Dirk mustered enough curiosity to amble into the living room and take a look at it. Then, with a sigh, he flopped down on the rug with it, shredded the wrappings, and proceeded to gnaw and ingest the big cookie. We didn't realize it then, but a tradition had been born, at least in Dirk's mind.

With the exception of the facts that everyone was a year older and the gifts were different, the next Christmas Day was a rerun of every previous December 25 in our dog's life. But this time, as the gifts were being handed around and opened, he was very alert, and after awhile, he became quite agitated. He began to bounce up and down in the double doorway and emit sharp little yips. Family members asked, "What's the matter, Dirk?" and "Are you hungry?" "Thirsty?" No. Finally, after a short conference during which we decided that the county dogcatcher surely wouldn't be working on Christmas Day, the front door was opened and our dog was given the invitation he had never expected to hear in his life: "Want *out*, Dirk? Want to go *outdoors*?" No. Instead of the excited yelps and headlong rush to the door that we expected, he stayed where he was, bouncing and pleading.

It was Chris who had the memory and perception to figure out what he wanted. He said, "I bet he's waiting for a present! I gave him my gingerbread man last year, remember?" The rest of us declined to believe that the dog attached any more importance to that cookie than to any of the numerous other cookies he had been offered during the year. But Chris sneaked around to the kitchen, got one of the heavy lard-fried "sinkers" the old lady next door traditionally sent over every year for our Christmas breakfast, wrapped it in tissue paper with a ribbon rosette on top, and unobtrusively stuck it in the tree branches. A few gifts later, he plucked it out and loudly announced, "*Why, here is a present for DIRK!!*" Oh, with what relieved joy and importance our dog pranced into the center of the living room, received *his gift*, plumped down on the rug with it between his paws, and happily ripped the paper off! Then he reveled in every crumb of the very same doughnut he had refused to even taste in the morning. After he had finished it, he was content to sit peacefully among us and watch the rest of the proceedings.

Every year thereafter, we regularly forgot that he was expecting to get a present and every year he regularly reminded us in the same way. "What's the matter with the fool dog anyway?" "*Oh, m'gosh, we forgot to give him a present again!*" Someone would be dispatched to wrap up *something* and the once a year ritual would be re-enacted. In spite of the fact that he usually preferred that we should live our lives in our way, while he lived his in his way, we came to realize that there was one family festival in which he wished to participate, and that he cared enough to remember from year to year with definite expectations.

The Old Con
or
The Recidivist

Chapter Eight

It was inevitable that the most notorious scofflaw in town would occasionally run afoul of the dogcatchers and be hauled off to the pokey. Dirk even made things easy for them. At some point, he developed a passion for riding in cars, although it's hard to understand why as the only places he ever got to go in cars were (1) back home to his tie-out chain; (2) to the vet; (3) to the "holding tank" at the City garage; or (4) to the Pound, at Mason, the County seat. It was fifteen miles to the Pound, so perhaps he thought the nice, long ride was worth spending a couple of days or so in the randy company of other vagabonds before one of the Hogg people appeared to redeem him once again.

He enjoyed riding in cars so much that for a long time, all a driver – any driver – had to do was open the passenger-side door and holler, "Hey Dirk! Wanna ride?" and he would bound in to sit on the seat, just like he thought he was actually going somewhere. Andy was usually the one that set off to look for him, and he always made it worthwhile for Dirk by driving to the end of High Street and around the Legion Hall parking lot a few times before he brought him back.

The cops soon learned Dirk's weakness. Usually they just brought him home where, after giving us a brief description of the behavior that had brought him to their attention this time, they would plead, "See if you can't keep him tied up, *please?*" Sometimes, depending on the seriousness of the latest misdeed or depending on the cop, he would be taken to the City garage, and put in a padlocked pen, to be transferred to the Pound's paddy wagon as soon as the County dogcatcher could be summoned. Even then, one of the other cops might call for us to come and get him.

One time, this turned into another of the embarrassing situations he was so good at bringing about. Vick was the Mayor during an extremely stressful time in City politics. The City Manager had resigned, confidently expecting that the City Council would refuse to accept his resignation, and that the populace would rise up in indignation and start a petition to recall the Mayor. The Mayor and the Council accepted the resignation, and nothing else happened – at that point.

The Police Chief had been in close cahoots with the City Manager, and while all the unpleasantness was a-building, he had done his best to make sure that the Hogg family was adhering to every City ordinance to the last jot and tittle. During this time, Andy turned sixteen, got his driver's license, and quickly became the most careful teenage driver in the U.S. of A. Every time he backed out of the driveway, he had the City police car on his tail.

Besides hassling our teenagers and serving us with "blight notices" and weed-cutting summonses, we had heard through the City Hall grapevine that the Chief had one supreme goal, and that was to terminate the Mayor's dog. Then one fine day the word came to the Chief that Hogg's dog was in the holding pen. The Chief was not going to wait for the Pound wagon to come and get Dirk. He intended to take our mutt personally to the Pound and order his immediate execution as a Public

Nuisance, Career Criminal, Incorrigible Vagabond, and perhaps as a Sex Maniac. The Chief was sure that the Mayor would be devastated, of course.

As an unpopular Head of the Law in town, along with his involvement in several other local and City administration feuds, the Chief was at bitter cross-purposes with the Superintendent of Public Works. As coincidence would have it, this man was the father of the girl who had given Franny our dog, and he, of course, recognized Dirk. He also had a key to the pen's padlock. The errant dog was freed in a trice, and bade, "Git!! Go home!" which Dirk was happy to do, as it was time for supper, and he may have had some uneasy premonition that this time things might turn out to be a bit more serious than usual. Dirk trotted home and was duly tied up by his doghouse, with none of us the wiser, as he had only been gone about an hour, and we hadn't missed him.

For a couple of days, we were totally innocent of the unholy uproar caused by this little incident, but the accusations flew thick and fast, and the repercussions brought about some major departmental changes in a few months, besides giving folks something to talk about in a dull summer. In fact, the town went through three city managers, three police chiefs, and two public works superintendents in a chain of events that was traceable back to our catalyst dog.

In writing of Dirk's adventures, it may sound as if he was running free most of the time, but he wasn't. He managed to escape about once a month on average, but multiply twelve months by fourteen years, and it is obvious that he could have found a lot of interesting entertainment in approximately a hundred and seventy opportunities.

While I have no eyewitness accounts of any of the times that Dirk actually ended up in the hoosegow, I vividly recall one occasion when the animal control officer made an outstandingly valiant and beyond-the-call-of-duty attempt to arrest him. It was a day in early spring, and there was a foot or more of heavy, wet snow on the ground, with some much deeper drifts in our field on the riverbank. I spotted Dirk fleeing, if that is the right word for the strenuous efforts he was making to flounder through the neighbors' back yards toward our place. Just then, the Pound truck pulled up in front of our house and a determined animal control officer jumped out, brandishing a long pole with a noose on one end of it. Tim and I stepped out on the porch to call the pooch into the house, but he was heading into the field where he would have more room to maneuver. And the dogcatcher went after him.

Their slow-motion ballet probably looked to a casual observer as if the two of them were having a rollicking good time playing tag, and I think Dirk was – at first. For many long minutes, he lollopped through the deep snow, surfacing in porpoise-like leaps, alternating with dives when he disappeared into the drifts.

As for the County man, he wasn't having any fun from the beginning. It would seem that a man with good sense would have quit the chase after the first time or two he tripped over his pole-and-noose and did a belly flop in a snowdrift, but perhaps the fellow lacked that quality. He continued to scramble to his feet and plow a few feet further before he did another cold wet nosedive. It was a soundless confrontation; both the dog and the minion of the law were beginning to run out of lung capacity by then.

Up on our porch, one of the spectators was anything but soundless. Tim was jumping up and down alternately bellowing encouragements to Dirk and insults aimed at the dogcatcher. He taunted the hapless man with his lack of physical coordination, and made rude hints indicating that his maternal ancestry was closely related to Dirk's. I guess I wasn't actually silent either. I was energetically punching Tim's shoulder and hissing, "Shut up, Tim! *Shut UP!!!*" I always felt that there was nothing to be gained by making a tense situation tenser.

Dirk, tiring of a game that was getting seriously out of hand, made one last end run, thrashed through the yard and dashed up on the porch, where he plumped down between our feet, too winded for even one triumphant bark. As the officer struggled his way up through the field, he was also breathless, but he managed to gasp out a threat we had heard on a few other occasions, "*If -I -ever -see -that -dog -again -I'll -shoot -him!*"

Tim wasn't winded a bit, of course, and his indignation was aroused to a high pitch. He patted Dirk protectively as he lectured the dogcatcher in a voice that could be heard all over the neighborhood, on the fact that this was *our* property that *our* dog had been running around on, and that if the man did, indeed, shoot Dirk, he, Tim, would personally see that he was fired, and the County was sued. His voice went up a few decibels in a parting shot as the weary official, dragging his noose, clambered into his truck. "*–AND I S'POSE YOU GET A BIG BONUS EVERY TIME YOU GRAB SOMEBODY'S PET OFF THEIR PORCH!!!*"

I was so glad to get both boy and dog shoved into the house.

We never knew what Dirk had done to bring himself to the County Animal Control's attention that day. Perhaps the officer was just cruising with a truckload of miscreants when he saw a familiar mutt that he knew from experience was either up to no good, or planning on it. Actually, except for his admittedly annoying vagrant forays, which were sometimes combined with his quests as a gourmand, or his romantic adventures, Dirk really wasn't a bad dog. He never got in fights and chewed up somebody's lap dog, or killed their cats or other pets, and if he had ever bitten a human being or even threatened to, we would certainly have heard about it.

However, either this dogcatcher or one of his cohorts did manage to impound Dirk a few times. When that happened, if he hadn't freed himself to roam by chewing or squirming his way out of his current collar, the Pound could identify us as his owners by the numbers on his dog tags, and then they would call us to come and get him. But if he hadn't come home for a couple of days, Franny and Chris would drive down to the Pound to see if he was there.

If he were in the lockup, they would play a sadistic little game with him to try to impress on his independent soul that home was the best place to be. They would walk along the row of holding pens, saying to each other,

"Well, I don't see Dirk anywhere – do you Chris?" and, "No, I don't think he's here, Franny. I think we've lost him for good this time. But look, here's a friendly little fella – how are ya, boy? Would you like to come home with us and be our doggie?" And they would keep this up for awhile, until Dirk was beside himself, leaping against the grill door and pleading frantically, *"HERE I AM!! HERE I AM!!"* Then, after a few more tours, one of them would relent and say, "Oh, *here* he is! Wanna go for a ride, Dirk?"

Of course, he wanted to go for a ride. And after a few months to forget his last incarceration, he would be all too ready to respond to the next invitation by a Williamston cop. After all, what did he care? He knew that no matter where he ended up, Franny and Chris would always come and rescue him.

The Great Communicator

or

Dog As Linguist

Chapter Nine

A well-known Scottish evening prayer beseeches: "From ghoulies and ghosties and long-leggity beasties and things that go BOOMP in the night, may the good Lord deliver us."

And also deliver us from the dog that feels he has to tell us at length about each and every boomp and beastie. Our neighbor on the west, the landlady of the old house that had been remodeled into five apartments, never hesitated to call at any hour when Dirk developed a barking jag. Well, to be truthful, she wasn't the only one who complained, and we really couldn't blame them. He was an indefatigable yapper.

To excuse him to some extent, he seemed to have very poor vision, even for a dog, and the dense fringe of poodle hair that dangled in front of his face didn't help his eyesight. On a foggy night, he couldn't see much of anything, so he barked and barked and barked to warn off all murderous thugs and nameless amorphous creatures that he was sure were lurking just at the edge of his range of vision.

It was fairly easy to quiet him if he was tied up. We just brought him in the house and put him in the bathroom where he couldn't see anything outdoors that might set him off. But if he happened to be at large, he could drive the mildest souls in our neighborhood into a murderous fury. (These mild souls often included members of his personal family.)

One late night when the visibility outdoors was about twenty feet, he had been pirouetting under the streetlight boxing the compass with his maddening yaps for hours and showing no signs of getting tired of it. I got so mad I went outdoors in my nightgown and started throwing chunks of cement at him from an ample pile provided by a sidewalk we had just dug up. I was rewarded with a few sharp yelps that let me know I had connected, and as my aim improved, he began to get nervous. Finally, he trotted from the middle of the street into a hedge of tartarian honeysuckle that was between our yard and the apartment house.

There he continued screeching and I continued throwing cement at him, but the dense bushes were deflecting all my missiles. I would have been happy to kill him that night, and perhaps I was looking for a more effective weapon with which to do it, when I came into the house just in time to hear the phone ringing. It was about three o'clock in the morning and Vick had just picked up the phone in the kitchen. I was standing close enough to hear our landlady friend bellow, "What in hell is that goddam dog barking at this time of the night???"

And Vick, always unfailingly polite, answered, "Why, Ila, he's barking to keep the evil spirits away."

"WHAT?"

"And he's doing a good job, too. You haven't seen any around here lately, have you?"

A long, shocked, pause – and then SLAM!!!

I have to admit, though, that on rare occasions, he could have been trying to alert us to a sight that would have made anyone nervous. One murky night when he was in the house, in the wee hours of the morning, he suddenly went into such raving conniptions at the bay window that I got up to investigate. The surrealistic vision I saw by the dim streetlight between floating bands of fog stiffened the hairs on the back of my neck and on my arms. What appeared to be the vanes of a Dutch windmill mounted sideways on legs was twirling itself up High Street through the thick mist. And it was sort of singing in a muffled bonging way.

Before the apparition disappeared into the murk, I was able to make out the town's most lovable eccentric walking up the street, spinning two long house-painting ladders that were balanced on his shoulders. And he had a large bucket over his head, which was poking through the rungs. The music was emanating from that bucket.

I wasn't sure whether I was happy that Dirk had awakened me or not. On the one hand, I knew that I had witnessed a once-in-a-lifetime phenomenon. On the other hand, it was quite awhile before I could get back to sleep.

Usually, in people/animal communications, the animals have to be the interpreters. Any domesticated creature, sheep, cow, horse, or household pet, is expected to learn and obey a lot of commands in the language of its owners. Even dimwits like chickens learn, "C'mere, chick-chick-chick," and "Shoo!" However, people seldom bother to learn the language of barks, mews and whinnies. This had always seemed unfair to me, as humans are supposed to be the more intelligent species. Cats are born with the knowledge that they are "kitties," and if coached, will easily learn their given names and several other words that have some bearing on their individual hedonistic and laid-back lifestyles. Dogs, of course, can be taught to understand a great many words and commands. Indeed, many dogs are heartbreakingly anxious to learn people language so they can demonstrate their empathy and obedience toward their masters and earn the coveted accolade, "Good DOG!"

But not all dogs are like that.

Dirk knew he was a "dog" and that it was not a complimentary term, at least in the context he most often heard it, "Oh, you dog, you!!" In fact, when someone referred to him as a dog even in a pleasantly conversational way, he always ducked his head, assumed a dejected posture, rolled his eyes at the speaker, and stuck his tongue out a little bit, by which actions he plainly communicated, "Oh, please forgive me for being a lowly despised creature, but I can't help being a dog, you know!"

By the time he was fourteen years old, Dirk had learned a lot of English words that one wouldn't expect to find in a dog's vocabulary, but they had special connotations for him. We weren't sure how many words he understood, but we knew we had to be very careful of what we said if he was within earshot. Of course, many dogs can interpret, "Are you planning to take him out to the *vet* today?" and "He really has to have a *bath*," in time to take some evasive action. And conversely, casual remarks such as "I'm going down to *play ball* in the *park*," or, "I bought some *candy*. It's in the cupboard," will bring on ear-flapping ecstasies in any mutt with a normal IQ.

But there were times when we really had to wonder at the range of Dirk's vocabulary. One quiet evening – we didn't have many of those – Vick and I were sitting on the sofa sort of watching a TV show, but he was also reading a book, and I, with my sewing basket beside me, was mending kid clothes. Occasionally, we exchanged quiet remarks. Dirk was companionably sitting between us, half snoozing, with his brain apparently totally disengaged. Both of us happening to glance at him at the same time, our minds, which often ran in the same groove, noted the thick ragged clump of poodle hair on his shoulders, working its way loose. With no inflection that could possibly have alarmed any creature, I said, "That's ridiculous," and Vick said, "Hand me your scissors and I'll fix it." But at the word "scissors", our dog gently oozed himself off the sofa and through the door.

And one time when Dirk had liberated himself, but was running around in our yard, Tim went outdoors with a slice of cheese with which to lure him within arm's range. I was watching them from the open kitchen window. Tim was sitting on the grass and seemed to be carrying on a conversation with the dog. Soon Dirk walked up to him, took the cheese, and flopped down in the grass to eat it. Tim kept on talking to him and petting him, and I said, very quietly so as not to alert the pooch, "Tim, grab him," but he didn't and Dirk immediately dashed out of the yard.

Frustrated, I hollered, "Why didn't you get him when you had the chance?" and Tim said indignantly, "Mom, I told him I had a piece of cheese for him, and I wasn't going to tie him up! Why, if I'd broken my promise and grabbed him, he wouldn't have believed anything I told him ever again!"

Dirk and the Hogg Kids

or

Porcupines, Postmen, and Floozies

Chapter Ten

If the Hogg siblings were engaged in one of their many creative enterprises at home, Dirk would stick around just to watch developments. Quite often, he would witness happenings that were outside the usual canine experience, and sometimes he got to play a bit part. There were even occasions when his bit part became the prime role.

When Andy was fifteen years old, he was a model member of the Boy Scouts of America. He was as diligent, eager, and hardworking in that organization as he was indiligent and dilatory in school classes, where he daydreamed through the hours, doing just enough work on his lessons so he wouldn't have to repeat the class the next year. He lived for his free hours and vacations when he could concentrate on the really important stuff, like fixing engines, and dipping into all sorts of pursuits and areas of expertise via earning Scout merit badges.

Eventually, he was inducted into the Order of the Arrow, a Scout honor society. Our O.A. Scouts had an Indian dance team that put on exhibitions and attended Indian pow-wows around the State. Of course Andy was excited about dressing up as an Indian; he was a sucker for uniforms. Sometimes we wondered it that was the real reason he became a Scout in the first place. A few years later, he joined a kilted bagpipe band, and then, in 1972, it may have been the traditional uniform that lured him into enlisting for four years in the U.S. Navy.

Besides learning the dance steps and their meanings, the boys in the O.A. had to make their own dance costumes. The Troop had books that showed how to fabricate the details to make their outfits look authentic. Depending on the type of costume they had chosen, the boys made "eagle" feather headdresses, finger-wove elaborate "assumption sashes", made little jingle cones out of tin lids to fasten on the ends of leather fringes, and wove headbands on beadwork looms. To make his dance costume, Andy even bought an ancient treadle sewing machine that he fitted out with a leather needle, after I flatly refused to let him burn out the motor on my sewing machine making his leather garments.

In the rear of our van, Andy kept a shovel and a plastic trash bag just in case he happened on any likely road kills that he could utilize parts of to enhance his Indian image. The prize corpse would be that of a porcupine. Then he could dye the quills different colors and embroider Chippewa flowers on his moccasins and loincloth. He could have bought beautifully prepared quills in a craft shop, but that wouldn't have been the Hogg Way. And one summer day, when our family was driving down from a trip to the Straits of Mackinac, it came to pass that there was a recently mashed porcupine on the freeway. Drivers were supposed to stop only for emergencies, but Andy's indulgent father stopped, and with the approbation of everybody in the car but his mother, Andy swiftly leaped out, shoveled the porcupine remains into his bag, and we were on our way again.

After we were home, as Andy prepared to skin his trophy, I gave him a lecture on stashing the stretched and curing hide somewhere where animals or little kids couldn't get at it. I think I suggested the steep garage roof, as being not only the most inaccessible site, but also it would place the hide out of smelling range of the house. My recollection is that he agreed to that plan.

A couple of days later, from the kitchen window, I saw our dog standing quietly in the side yard with his mouth open, but he wasn't barking. As I watched him, I noticed his tongue was sticking out a bit, and he seemed to be uncomfortable about something. When I went out to investigate, I had to get within a couple of feet of him before I saw that there were porcupine quills all around his mouth mixed in with his grizzled curly hair, and that the protruding part of his tongue was skewered with countless quills.

The blinding rage that overwhelmed me then makes me an unreliable narrator for what happened next, but I know I tore through the house and environs until I found and rousted Andy from whatever pursuit he was engaged in. I grabbed a pair of needle-nose pliers, and ordered Andy to hold the dog perfectly still and then I ordered the dog to stand perfectly still while I pulled the quills out of him, and I bellowed at both of them every time Dirk even twitched.

Andy says I was making threats and calling them names the whole time in language and a tone of voice that scared him, as I was using terms he had no idea that a mother would even know. Apparently I had been saving them up for the right occasion. Well, he should have been scared. I was getting madder by the minute as I told him to hold Dirk's jaws open so I could pull out the hundreds of quills in the roof of his mouth. I do remember yanking the dog's slobbery tongue out as far as it would go, and gripping it with one hand while I de-quilled it with the other.

After the ordeal was over and Dirk was tied up by his doghouse – although I think he would have been happy to stay out there without being tied that day – I went in search of the porcupine hide. Of course Andy knew where it was. Nicely scraped and heavily salted, I found it nailed out on the top of an old crate by the garage, where it was all of three feet off the ground. Our idiot cur had eaten about a third of it. When I saw that, if there were any words applicable to the situation that I hadn't used yet, I'm sure I used them then.

I don't know what happened to the rest of the porcupine hide, but Andy made sure to put it some place where I would never lay eyes on it again. There were still plenty of quills left on it. Perhaps he did dye them and work them into his outfit, but if he did, he didn't feel it was worth the risk to point out his handiwork to me.

Generally, Dirk wasn't much interested in the boys' pastimes, which consisted mostly of such projects as making three junkyard rejects into one runnable car. Girls were usually up to more interesting pursuits, to Dirk's mind. And one summer, we had a lot of girls around. There was Franny, of course, and also Cathy, our niece from Kansas. Nancy, who was working part time for us, lived in a downstairs apartment in the rambling old house next door. In theory, the girls were busy with college classes in Lansing or painting our house, but in retrospect, they seem to have had quite a bit of unstructured time on their hands. Whenever they were around, Dirk, even if unchained, preferred hanging around with them to scaring up fun on his own.

One of the girls' ongoing projects was the seducing of "Happy Howie, the Hippy Postman" away from "the swift completion of his appointed rounds." Although Howie always wore the prescribed summer uniform of blue shorts, short-sleeved shirt, knee socks and cap, his long ponytail and earrings weren't exactly "regs." He was a beginning mail carrier, and that summer was the probationary period to see if he had the right stuff to make a career in the U.S. Postal Service. Thanks, at least in part, to our girls, he didn't make the grade. I hope they still feel some guilt for what they did to that fine young man, but they probably don't.

A different girl would sit on the front steps with Dirk every afternoon at mail time, waiting for Howie. Dirk had none of the dark prejudice the normal pooch develops against a man in uniform carrying a bag up the porch steps and *doing something* to the front door every day. He was always glad to greet any visitor except another dog. The girl would engage Howie in flirtatious repartee for as long as she could tease him into sticking around. It was a contest to see who could keep him there the longest. I don't remember who won, but I seem to recollect that the winning time was about two and a half hours. People living half a block from our house on either side could clearly see Howie standing there, gabbing. Inside two weeks, everybody on the street knew where the bottleneck was, and they would call our house when they got impatient. At the time, I was spending most of the day working at our museum display studio downtown, but if I happened to be home when one of those calls came in, I would step to the door with an urgent errand in mind that could only be done by the appointed siren-of-the-day. Then Happy Howie, with a debonair farewell, would take up his burden, fling his ponytail back over his shoulder, and stride off up the street.

Besides beguiling Howie on the front porch, the girls also harassed a young man from the rear of our house. His name was Tom, and he lived in the upstairs back studio apartment next door. Somewhere I have pictures the girls took of each other the day they dressed up to go over and vamp Tom. They are wearing mini-skirts and very off-the-shoulder peasant blouses, day-glo makeup, fake eyelashes, and voluminous rump-length blonde wigs. The landlady, who also lived in one of the upstairs apartments, was uncharacteristically at a loss for words when she saw them come tripping up the back hall stairs in high heels with Dirk, who had gift bows stuck all over him and bright red polish on his toenails. All she could come up with was, *"I always knew you were floozies!"* and *"Git that goddam dog out of my house!"*

Everybody living on the east side of the apartment house could see the five-foot-long telescope the girls had set up poking out of one of our upstairs windows, trained on Tom's window. As it was an astronomical telescope, it didn't focus very well at twenty yards, and of course anything happening over there was happening upside down to the viewer at the eyepiece. But Tom, like Howie, seemed to be flattered rather than upset by all the attention.

Sometimes the girls went swimming, taking Dirk with them. As it wasn't "cool" to swim in the municipal pool, and anyway, you couldn't take your dog in with you there, they went to "The Pit," an abandoned clay mine on the east edge of town. It was over ninety feet deep, and ice-cold springs kept it filled. It was posted "No Swimming" but who paid any attention to that? One evening, walking the half mile back home, it occurred to the girls to give the folks in passing cars along the way a little drama to pique their imagination and possibly even get a car or two to run off the road. The girls rolled their swimsuit tops down and bottoms up, and arranged their towels to cover any vestige of swimwear. With their bare feet and wet hair, they appeared to have been swimming in the altogether when a dastardly practical joker made off with their street clothes. On the sidewalk, they hid behind trees and bushes, peering around with exaggerated caution before they made the dash to the next tree. They had the satisfaction of hearing brakes squeal, and seeing car passengers and home dwellers crane their necks to ogle them all along the way.

They also did the tuck-up-the-shorts and pull-down-the-shoulders bit when they undertook some "interpretive dancing" in our little field. Nancy had borrowed the white net curtains from the picture window in her apartment, and they arrayed themselves in these filmy draperies. With more net curtains as floating veils, they became barefoot woodland nymphs cavorting in a dreamy glade by the river's edge. Dirk, happy to be a part of this unique cultural event, had one of the "veils" fastened to his collar, and a wreath of Queen Anne's Lace around his neck.

As the girls postured and leaped and high-kicked in the tall grass, and the dog bounced and yapped, they were all making glorious fools of themselves. Swirling their veils in a graceful measure, they became aware, too late, that Vick was standing on our dock, talking to a stranger. The girls were momentarily flustered, but he wasn't. With his typical unflappable poise, he formally introduced each girl to the important client he was courting that day. I don't remember if he got that job or not.

Another dull summer weekend afternoon, Dirk was the star, and of course, he knew it. The girls dressed him up in an old sweater and everything else they could think of to make him look outlandish, including a G.I. Joe doll tied on his back with a bandana. The contest, this time, was to see who could parade him through the park where a big family reunion was going on, and not crack a smile no matter how people reacted. The contest was over almost as soon as it began. Dirk trotted to the center of the group, pranced around proudly in his finery before the astonished family, and then squatted and relieved himself in their midst.

The girls didn't stick around to hear any remarks; they sprinted for home.

Curtains

or

Is He Still Out There?

Chapter Eleven

After Dirk returned home apparently nearly lamed for life by his fruitless efforts to sire a new dog breed that would have astonished the world – half cockerpoo and half St. Bernard – he seemed to be happy lying around on the porch for days while he was convalescing. We thought maybe his advanced age was beginning to catch up with him, and he would finally be content to slow down and become a peaceful companion within the Hogg family bosom. But that was not to be.

It seemed that one day he was still having a hard time negotiating the porch steps, and the next, he was up and running, and off into the wild blue yonder. For two or three days, we had no news of him and then one afternoon, a neighbor child reported that he was down in the park playing with some kids. We assumed that he would be hungry and tired, as was usual after one of his jaunts, and would come home at suppertime to eat and rest from his latest escapade. But he never showed up and we never saw him again.

And we never found out what happened to him. We thought if he had been snatched by the County vagabond patrol, they would have got his number off his license tags and called us, as they had numerous times before. But perhaps he did make his final car ride in the Pound paddy wagon. A couple of months later, I was somewhat shaken when I found his tags in a cluttered buffet drawer. Apparently they had never been reattached to his last new collar. I knew that after that length of time, he would have suffered the ultimate penalty. Perhaps especially if they had recognized him as one of their most frequent boarders, they might not have gone to extraordinary lengths to try to identify him and his family.

But there were so many other ways that could have been the means by which he was transported to the Big Doghouse in the Sky. For instance, he could have been so engrossed in scraping a flat rabbit off the highway that he hesitated a fraction of a second too long as a semi barreled down the asphalt toward him. And considering all the threats to shoot him that we had personally heard voiced and the amount of shot already under his hide, a good case could be made that a maddened gunman with better aim than the others had finally managed to hit a vital spot.

Even a year or more after he disappeared, family members confessed that they still felt a few heart flutters if, when driving along a country road, they happened to see a pile of something shaggy and dark, about his size, in a ditch. On closer investigation, it always turned out to be a torn black trash bag, or a ragged old bath mat or coat.

Life proceeded at its normal hectic pace at Hoggwilde, but it seemed to have lost some of its piquant flavor. It was duller, more adult, more responsible. The Hogg kids were pulling up stakes and leaving the parental manor in pickup trucks loaded with about half of their worldly goods. The other half they left behind, just in case, stuffed in the attics or stowed under their beds. They were staying away for ever longer intervals, and each time they left home, it was for a further distant destination.

Eventually, they scattered far: Andy, in his sailor suit, to the Mediterranean and in and out of Virginia Beach on an aircraft carrier; Franny, in hippy garb, to California colleges, and a pre-law degree in Political Science; Chris, in dungarees and boots, to the archaeological digs and museum work at the Straits of Mackinac; Tim, to Grand Haven on Lake Michigan as production manager of a factory. Vick and I were still at home, in an otherwise empty ten-room house on two overgrown acres, writing reports and fabricating history museum exhibits in our downtown studio. We didn't get another dog. We still had a couple of the old cats, and they were lonesome, too.

Occasions when the Hogg kids were all home at the same time became very rare, but when they were all together, and the new adventures had been told and exclaimed over, the old ones would surface. And it was surprising how many of them began, "Do you remember the time when Dirk —?" It seemed as if the retold adventures that put everyone in stitches were the ones that had most exasperated and embarrassed us when they happened. Sooner or later, the talk would turn to theories about our dog's final fate, including the fanciful notion that he could still be alive, unlikely as that would be, ten years after a fourteen-year-old dog's disappearance. But whenever and however Dirk's busy life came to an end, we had to admit that in the tapestry of our lives as a family, the wild threads he wove, like it or not, left us a colorful legacy that none of our dozens of other pets could match.

pmh

Epilogue

But – what if – on his last ramble, he so charmed some nice family with lots of children that they lured him home with them and adopted him? And they have kept him ever since in a really, truly escape-proof – but luxurious – kennel. There, all these long years, he waits like an enchanted prince in a fairy tale for the moment when someone is a bit careless about locking the kennel gate. Then he'll be *free*! And off down the road like a little fuzzy black tumbleweed, he'll come racing back to us, as fast as the wind can blow him!

And this time, he'll be home to stay.

A Dog Called Dirt